Aronnax: A Tale of Twenty Thousand Leagues

WRITTEN BY TONY LAPLUME

ISBN: 9798534475081

TO THE ENGLISH DEPARTMENT OF
THE UNIVERSITY OF MAINE, ORONO

Post-collegiate life, especially if you drift far away from the schooling environment, can sometimes leave a large gulf from the life one knew on campus. Working on this project has helped remind me that it's only as far as I let it.

CONTENTS

ACKNOWLEDGMENTS

This story happens at all because Kindle originally rejected an earlier project, and then Kindle introduced its Vella program, which motivated this one.

JULIAN, OR TWENTY THOUSAND LEAGUES IN THE BACKYARD

The thing about being a kid is that people are always going to underestimate you, and by "people" I mean everyone, and by "everyone" I mean even your own parents. Mine, anyway. And specifically, my dad.

Well, as of a few months ago my dad began to regret that. He was diagnosed with lung cancer, and the prognosis gave him what he took to be an alarmingly short amount of time in which to put his affairs in order. Naturally, nobody wants me to know exactly how much time that is, especially him, so I assume the worst. I assume he'll be dead by the end of the year.

So I have complicated feelings about all this. He never really made the time for me, and when he did, he didn't seem much interested. He's one of those people who could get along with anyone, and basically everyone loved him, and you felt privileged to know him. But that apparently stops if he doesn't know how to make that connection, if the audience is hard to gage. I'm like that. I'm pretty much the opposite of him in personality. I don't talk much, and it's not easy for everyone to get along with me, and I don't suppose everyone loves me. Maybe it'll change. Maybe I'll figure all that out.

It'll have taken too long. It took too long in my own house. Fourteen years or so. Long enough to be sure. I mean, childhood is pretty long, far longer than it seems. Parents will know long before even the first year is over, will already have set the terms of the relationship. I have friends with younger siblings. These are things you notice. I can only imagine the disappointment my dad felt, and how long things have dragged out for him.

Somehow, I've gotten around it, and by "somehow" I mean that I've filled up my time nicely, made an entire world of the world around me, which is to say, I've taken advantage of the possibilities that might be considered background material for a lot of other people.

Take the submarine in the backyard, for example.

It's yellow and it's covered in graffiti. It's been there forever. For a lot of other people, it's just there, just a piece of junk to be *treated* as junk. To me, it's everything. I never had a clubhouse, a tree fort, except this submarine, this rusting, aging, abandoned, trashed, derelict relic of the ancient past (relatively speaking) that was here long before I was born, before even my parents or grandparents were born, in the backyard of a house that has been in the family for generations, at least a hundred years, crowded in the confines of Woonsocket, Rhode Island.

To reach it, because when I say "backyard" I don't mean immediately behind my house, but down a fairly steep but short hill, I always had to be careful, which is the one thing I distinctly remember my dad telling me, over and over again, from a very young age. He always thought I would break my neck tripping and tumbling down.

The submarine has been there so long anyone with any memory of it outside the family died long ago, and nobody else seems to have cared to commemorate it. There's no plaque, no history marker, no sign that gives an indication that it's worth anything at all, but the one thing my dad always made sure I knew was that it *was* valuable, not just in general, but to my family in particular.

Sorry, allow me to make a proper introduction:

My name is Julian Aronnax, and I am the descendant of Pierre Aronnax. That name might not mean anything to you, but if you have ever heard of Captain Nemo, it's because of him.

This is to say, the submarine in my backyard is Captain Nemo's; it is the Nautilus.

Now, my dad always had his hobby of working on cars, restoring them, detailing them, maintaining them, waxing them, you name it. He was always working on one car or another. It never really interested me, and I guess you probably know why. When the diagnosis happened, he made a radical decision: He wanted to restore the submarine. He wanted to resurrect the Nautilus. And he wanted my help.

I couldn't believe it. I almost refused him on the spot. This would have been bad, as it was in the hospital, and he lay there in the bed with an IV running out of his arm, machines beeping behind him, mom crying, me crying, him crying, everyone pretty convinced that he had *days* not *weeks* or *months*, much less *years*.

In that moment he was very small indeed, but he made a declaration that was enormous. He said he could do it, and that he needed my help.

I hesitated. I hesitated for a brief moment, but it felt like an eternity. Then I told him that I would. I decided not to underestimate the unexpected opportunity that had presented itself. This was going to be a family thing, in ways that might shock the whole world, all over again. An Aronnax tradition.

PIERRE, OR AN INTERNATIONAL MYSTERY

The story of Pierre Aronnax perhaps begins with a Polish woman named Krystyna Ciszek, who married Pierre late in the nineteenth century, after the events that informed his life and defined his family for generations had already occurred. Pierre and Krystyna met not in his native France or her Poland, but in America, where they had separately decided to settle after decidedly unsettled lives had left them yearning for a semblance of security. They met not far from the grounds of the house where the Aronnax family has lived ever since, in fact. My dad, and this is one of the many things that until now I have never really appreciated, used to point out the exact spot every time we passed it in our travels around the city.

The Poland of Krystyna's day was beset with Russian intrigue, a story that is itself not very hard to understand. She grew up in a household with a brother she never named, but whose identity formed the intense bond she was to have the rest of her life with Pierre, for he was the man who subsequently adopted the identity of Nemo. Pierre's France forbade him to have any part in Poland's struggles, until fate delivered him at the metaphorical doorstep of the last and greatest of its patriots. In fact, had Pierre been allowed to pursue certain lines of inquiry regarding the emerging mystery, he might have known everything from the start.

As such, in July of 1866, he and the rest of the world entered the mystery with a blank slate after the first reports of a rampaging oceanic entity began to circulate. Pierre was a marine biologist of some renown, much-respected and -consulted, and well-versed in traveling abroad to assist and investigate as he pleased, an ordinary adventurer much used to life at sea, which at this point in history was still an affair not to be taken lightly but receding into the hidden past of extraordinary dangers. Nearly fifty years earlier there had been a much-discussed maritime disaster that produced a work of fiction thirty years later, concerning the obsessive hunt for a white whale, from a writer previously best known for his contributions to the exotic explorations of cannibal civilizations, and not much called-upon for more. Pierre was one of the few eager readers of that work, concerned as he was in identifying all the creatures of the deep, separating the real from the imagined. In those times, it was still possible to confuse the two. The kraken of myth, for instance, still haunted men's dreams, and even the unicorn could still be evoked, on land, as if it might prance in broad daylight. Today we have fantastic beasts such as the Loch Ness Monster and Bigfoot, but only the truly determined, and none mainstream, believe them to be real. In Pierre's day, in more innocent times and yet so much more vivid, at the start of this story the American Civil War scarcely completed a year in the past, his was the task of setting up the boundaries, once and for all, of our modern world.

And so only a few days after the first encounter, another occurred, and then a few weeks later, two more, and then a deluge, six in all on a single day. Pierre is busy about his work, on an escapade he might have believed to be of some significance at the time, a worthy use of his time, and then he sticks his head out and there is six months of heated chatter concerning these encounters, the rough beast causing so much havoc, elusive, massive, like nothing seen before, and suddenly all those legends are real again, or worse, and Pierre finds himself, predictably, called to weigh in. A wizened perspective, his word is taken for what it's worth, an expert's opinion, and yet, no one knows what to do, and just as suddenly as it appeared, the entity vanishes.

In the opening months of 1867, it's as if none of it had happened at all, and all the heated passions cooled, all motivation to action lost. Tempers flare easily, but given time all men favor caution. Well, most. A few remain excitable, and their voices loud, so that it can sometimes prove difficult to tell the difference, and perspective is hard to find. Usually it needs painful reminder to rouse interest again, and that's exactly what happens in March, and then in April an alarming report of irrefutable urgency. Pierre has just arrived in New York, and as it happens a ship by the name of *Abraham Lincoln* is packing for the long-awaited pursuit of this mystery, under the command of Captain Farragut.

Pierre has with him his faithful assistant Conseil, and meets a fabled harpooner named Ned Land as he answers a summons to assist Farragut. And just like that, the hunt begins.

ELLE, OR THE GIRL WHO GETS AWAY

I met Julian a long time ago, in ancient days, after I moved to town in elementary school. Boys were old enough to be complete jerks. One even stuck a worm in my hair! But they were stupid little boys who had no idea how to respond to a cute girl.

To be fair, we're just about to finish middle school, and boys aren't really any better. Except my boyfriend. And Julian.

Everyone always knew Julian was a little different. He never really knew how to fit in, maybe not weird enough to be considered weird, but he didn't really have social skills. He'd make time for David, who was developmentally disabled, and for some that was excuse to treat Julian with just this side of ridicule. They thought he wasn't growing up fast enough.

Well, like I already suggested, boys are hardly the best judge of character. They always overestimate themselves, and underestimate everyone else. I never had time for them.

The truth is, I never really had time for Julian, either, but he's the kind of boy who if you bump into him, you want to be nice to him. I did, anyway. He was nice. Shy, sure, although maybe he just didn't want to talk so much, or maybe he didn't know how, or maybe he just wasn't interested. Like I said, weird.

So when I'd see him in the hall, at the lockers, I'd be nice to him. He wasn't even weird about my boyfriend. He just took it as a fact of life and moved on. I'm sure there was a part of him that wished for some different outcome, but he seemed cool with it, and, well, all the other boys were a lot worse about it.

Anyway, all this is to say that everything would've been a lot easier if all I ever did was see Julian at school, and I could say that, but it wouldn't be the truth. Me and my boyfriend used to spend time hanging out around that stupid submarine. It's a town joke. If you listen around, it really should just be dismantled and tossed into a scrapyard. Everyone says so. Except Julian.

The one time I heard him speak with any passion at school was when someone uttered those very sentiments. It wasn't me, although naturally I didn't disagree. Julian, though, and he was immediately embarrassed, his face turning red, and his whole body folding inward, like a turtle, shouted, "No it's not."

And that's all he said. Coincidentally, I don't know, or maybe I just had never noticed, but not long after I saw him out around the submarine when me and my boyfriend were there again that weekend.

I told my boyfriend I wanted to talk to Julian, and walked over. Part of why all this worked out so well, this quasirelationship, was that even my boyfriend seemed cool with Julian, not in a condescending, "oh, he's such a nerd he'll never be a problem" kind of way, but that he seemed to get Julian in the same way I did, which I guess is why we were so compatible in the first place.

"Hey," I said. "So I guess this dumb old thing is important to you?"

Julian just kind of shrugged. It seemed like he wasn't going to say anything at all, but then he smiled and said, "It's kind of a long story."

"That's okay," I said. "I have some time."

"It's a whole family thing," he said. "I don't even know how much of it would make sense."

"Well," I said. "If you ever change your mind." So I walked back over to my boyfriend, and part of me felt awful, because I hadn't gotten around to telling Julian that I'm transferring to a new school, a private one, in the fall. I probably won't be coming around to this stupid submarine again much longer. There might not be another chance.

So I walked back over and promised to find the time to hear about it, and that's how it started. A couple weeks later me and my boyfriend were there again and Julian came around with his dad, and they explained the project they had in mind.

That's how we got drafted into it.

CONSEIL, OR ADVICE ON HIGH PURSUIT

From Conseil's journal:

I was privileged to make the acquaintance of and secure employment under Pierre Aronnax some years ago. Pierre had already established his scientific credentials across Europe, a reputation that extended well beyond his French homeland, a keen mind that was capable of piercing the veil of the natural world in a century of such discovery both fantastic (the dinosaur bones being excavated in a series of miracles, revealing the shape of ancient history such as had never been conceived) and incredible (Darwin's investigations into evolution on remote islands). Pierre's work was of a subtler kind, filling museums and laboratories, classrooms and the parlors of discerning gentlemen with the sort of physical evidence that had become a universal mania. He would undertake expeditions at the slightest suggestion☐, never seeking glory (he was no Schliemann!), and yet the biggest moment of his career fell in his lap when the greatest mystery of the age was set to be solved by a crew setting sail in the very New York harbor in which he had just docked, his cargo laden with fresh treasures waiting to be catalogued.

As I have suggested, I was very much eager to take part in such a career. In my native Belgium, I was a humble man content to solve minor mysteries, of a more immediate nature. Unofficially, I would assist in the investigation of crimes, often upon request, as my insight often helped to solve them. I prefer resolution above all else, an order to the cosmos, and find myself unsettled if I have a thought as to how this might be accomplished, but I never presumed to have a mind capable of accomplishing all of this on my own. I always sought out those better qualified for such work, and in Pierre Aronnax discovered someone eminently so.

I took on work as a simple assistant, and soon enough proved indispensable in that role. There was nothing I wouldn't do for Pierre. Somehow he always underestimated how far that instinct went, but in the quest for the mysterious beast haunting the world's oceans, he was to discover exactly that.

It was on June 2, 1867, in which Pierre received the summons to join the expedition to be launched under the command of Captain Farragut, aboard the *Abraham Lincoln*. He had little time in which to consider the request, the ship setting sail within a few hours. As I knew he would, he accepted instantly, the allure of the challenge too great for him, especially having been previously consulted on the matter and his notions being taken as expert opinion. Farragut struck me as a sober man equally capable of trusting in this venture, although I paid him little enough attention. I trusted Pierre to perform the task, and Farragut to facilitate him.

By the end of the month, we had settled into our voyage, consulting with a whaler concerning the mystery, while all still considered the object of our inquiry to be a natural one, very much the business of such enterprise. Our harpooner, Ned Land, proved to be the most skeptical, having the most experience in these matters, but none, much less Pierre, seemed interested in his opinion. In a few more days, having cleared a full month of pursuit, we rounded Cape Horn, and the crew remained in high spirits.

By the end of July we had crossed the equator, and a period of dismal cruising settled in, and hopes dwindled. We had nothing to see, nothing to analyze, no fresh sightings. Pierre always did his best work with physical evidence, after all, which is only to be expected, and in this adventure he had none of it. We were all seasoned seafarers, but the sea had shown us nothing except itself, and we had been keen for more, sure of our ability to discover the heart of the mystery. Where a fictional vessel had heard reports of its prey and its captain committed a disastrous but deliberate course, ours was real and fruitless.

At the start of November, Farragut at last admitted defeat and promised no more than three additional days before heading back, and it took the whole of the three days for Ned Land, of all people, to glimpse what we had come to see, only for Farragut to discover that whatever it was, it was far faster than the *Abraham Lincoln* could push itself, no matter how desperately he tried, straining its engines to beyond breaking point, when the completely unexpected occurred:

Pierre Aronnax fell overboard.

I at once observed this, and threw myself into the waters after him. I knew how little he had expected this, despite a certain period of years in our acquaintance in which I had done everything possible to assist him faithfully in all his interests, in his wild expression as he struggled for purchase, convinced he would drown, when my arms slipped around him. Never will I be more grateful than when I saw the look of relief spread across his face.

How such devotion as I exhibited then might happen was something even Pierre's keen mind couldn't fathom, and I still find it difficult to explain to others even now. The idea of the "faithful servant" is a popular, comforting one, to the point of willingness to sacrifice one's own life to maintain that of the master. That is not what motivated me that night.

Rather, it was my stubborn belief that the mystery still needed solving, and that Pierre Aronnax was the only person capable of doing so. The mystery itself had caused this predicament, and being so close to solving it spurred me on to unthinkable conclusions.

Unfortunately, my assistance alone was not going to be enough. We swam in a hapless fashion all night, and were on the verge of collapsing, when something even more unexpected occurred, and then something moreso after that...

JIMMY, OR A JOURNAL EXPLAINS EVERYTHING

I went to school with Julian, absolutely. I admit, I didn't really think much of him, but then again, nobody did. The guy seemed to go out of his way to be unlikeable. I don't mean that he smelled funny or had a weird personality. Actually, he *had* no discernible personality. This is to say, he was pretty hard to get to know. I'm not even sure he *had* friends. The longer I went to school with him, the rarer it was to see him hang out with anyone.

This was years ago, decades. Funny how time works. One minute you're in school and it seems to last an eternity, *each and every day*, and then you're out and you're getting a job, living an adult life that always seemed so mysterious when you were young but as it turns out is just like the life you knew as a kid, except now you've gotta take on all the responsibilities yourself...

Listen, I don't want to get into all that. This is about Julian. There's a lot I learned about him, later. For one, and I had no way of knowing this at the time, but when we *were* in school together, he somehow developed this whole mythology around *me*, around this one moment, this fight I had with another kid, someone *else* named Jimmy. That was Jimmy Franklin, the rare black kid in school. I don't even remember what the fight was about, probably just Jimmy Smith and Jimmy Franklin trying to prove how tough they were, same as any other fight.

Seems this incident left a huge impression on Julian. He started thinking about it so much he eventually misremembered it as "the fight between the two kids named Jimmy Smith, the white one and the black one." He wrote a lot of stories, and I guess the fight ended up showing up in them, and I would never have known anything at all about it except one day I ended up in possession of a notebook that as it turned out once belonged to Julian.

This isn't to say I wouldn't have given it back, if the opportunity had been there, but it wasn't. Julian moved out of town when he went off to college. Me, I never did. There's two kinds of people who don't leave their hometown: those who can afford to, and those who can't. I belonged in the latter. I was absolutely in that fight because I had something to prove.

Anyway, I can't really recall the exact circumstances of how the notebook ended up my possession, but it did. At first I thought it was an empty notebook, because it wasn't filled, not even remotely, and I guess I flipped past the pages Julian had scribbled in the first few times, just the first few pages.

Wait, I remember now. It was a flea market. I bought it in a flea market. You buy things at flea markets when you don't have a lot of money. You live with a lot of used things when you don't have a lot of money. Whatever works.

It sat in my apartment for years, even, after I acquired it, and I never thought much of it until I got married and had a kid, and one day, because I still don't have a lot of money, I came across this notebook and my kid comes up to me after school one day (he never gets into fights; sometimes history changes, slowly), and asks me to read the scribbling he says is in the notebook, and I say to him, "I have no idea what you're talking about." As far as I knew, the notebook had never been used. He opens it to the first page and says, "See? I can't read it." Neither could I, initially. Some people are completely illegible, and I guess Julian was one of them. So I sit there staring at the scratch marks for a while, and my kid joins in, and he's the one who finally starts figuring it out, of course.

It's the dates that stand out at first, before I see that it says, inside the front cover, "property of Julian Aronnax." I realize this is from back in the day, when *I* was in school! Life comes full circle, absolutely. I begin thinking about those days all over again. Nothing about Julian. There would've been no reason, at that point.

Then I start reading what turns out to be a journal. This is when I learn about the private life of one of the most private people I ever knew, or as it turned out, never knew at all. This is when I learn things that prompted me to start asking around town more about Julian, that stupid submarine, ancient history, even the hot girl who vanished without a trace just when us idiot kids started realizing what we had been missing.

I learned about some dude in the 19th century that went on a vendetta against basically the whole world because of how messed up it was, not stopping to think for a second that his approach wasn't exactly making anything better. I learned about another guy, Julian's ancestor, of all people, who survived encountering this maniac. I learned the submarine of that maniac had been rusting in my hometown for a hundred years. I learned that Julian and the hot girl actually thought they could fix the stupid thing and set it on another journey.

I learned they actually did it. I learned about Julian's dad. I wish I had never learned any of it. Sometimes you wish you'd known all about something, or someone, from the start, and then you wish you'd remained ignorant, because the truth is terrible, and beautiful, and heartbreaking, and you have no idea how knowing any of this makes your life, or the world, any better, because you wish everything had turned out better, and it just makes you wish *your own life* were better, that if that thing, or that person, had turned out better, there'd be hope for you, too.

I don't know. Maybe this whole thing is like knowing there was a kid who mixed up the circumstances of a fight he watched happening in school one time, something that leaves an impression that somehow, against all logic, makes the world a little better, and you don't really understand how or why, but that's the kind of stuff that makes life worth living.

A lot of people wish their lives were easier. Maybe it's not really about whether life is hard or easy. Maybe it's just the moments that give you perspective, if you can find them. Chances are, if you're lucky enough to find them, you'll like the story they have to tell.

Thank you, Julian.

NED LAND, OR THE HOOK

Ned Land, the man most likely to be found in this kind of situation, the one who would've been the star in most other versions, is the one with the most relevant experience, and the greatest ability to both challenge and accept what Pierre Aronnax found at the other end of his incredible journey.

There's a whole maritime tradition that unless you're born into it ends up feeling foreign, alien, even morally repugnant, as the idea of whaling was to become. If you are, though, you will most be signaled out by the accent you grow up around, whether you're a native of Nantucket, Boston, New York City, or the rocky coastline of Maine. This is to say, one of the first things Aronnax would've noticed about Ned was his accent. If you grow up on the water, you learn to clip your speech because it's highly unlikely you'll have a lot of time between crashing waves to make your point. This is why these accents tend to drops their "r"s, for instance.

To be a fisherman is to live with the constant awareness that those waves could very well pull you under permanently at any moment, the proverbial Davy Jones' Locker. Today we think mostly of pirates as the peril of the seas, but it was only ever really the waters themselves that yearned to claim the bodies of men, their ships, everything they had in this world, except the families they left behind.

Ned made his living like this. He sat there, that first day aboard the *Abraham Lincoln*, listening to the French professor's insane theories about the mythical beasts likely responsible for the shipwrecks they were set to investigate, and all he could do was keep a straight face and not shout aloud at what a lunatic he had found. He knew all about the professor's career, one of a whole legion of glory seekers who scoured land and sea, doing little actual hard work, accepting everything they saw and found at face value, and willing to believe any tall tale because it was all of this that funded their adventures, the gullible masses always far more interested in embellishment and the idea of expanding knowledge than learning concrete new truths.

Well, Ned lived with hard truths his whole life. He learned the art of harpooning the hard way, the family way, because he was born into it and had no other choice but to take it up, and *because* he grew up that way it was second nature by the time he was recruited by Farragut and encountered the professor on the sleek decks of the *Lincoln*.

He had little time for people who stood in awe of his abilities, but he didn't mind the slack attention when he let slip a harpoon, or spoke idly of confronting whales, which were stone cold killers to the layman, which might have been filled with oil but were hardly shy about smashing the hulls of ships they came across. The professor thought, generously, their target to be a narwhal, but it would've had to have been of the magnitude of a new world record for the species to affect the catastrophic damage left in its wake from all those alarming reports.

Ned took it all in stride.

He spent day and night casually, even better than the experienced crew of the *Lincoln*, so that Farragut himself glared in envy when he thought Ned wasn't looking. Farragut had a fine military background, so few years removed from the horrors of the Civil War. Privately, Ned yearned to discuss with the captain his true suspicions, as only Farragut might comprehend, but he could see only the fanatic in the man's eyes, the same as everyone else aboard.

No, Ned Land was a realist. At certain times realists are forced to become what they abhor most: alarmists. The dawn of the submarine was already decades in the past. If their object was such a thing, it would only be possible if it were in the magnitude of many times in advance of the most sophisticated submarine yet devised. And this scared Ned, to even consider.

It meant that at the end of this voyage was a fanatic of an equally inexpressible magnitude.

So he sat and listened to the professor rave about unicorns at sea, and did not laugh in his face, and squinted into the fathoms for long stretches at a time, the silent waters, so hungry, as no layman could ever conceive, hoping that he would not be the one to find their object, and he gloried in their failure for many months, a small drop in the bucket in the career of Ned Land in the mighty oceans of the world, and while the others despaired at the failure to discover their monster, he feared *finding it*.

He knew, all along, that it was his destiny to do exactly that. He cried out, the alarm mostly for his soul, when he saw it. Farragut ordered pursuit, the professor eager in his peculiar arts, which Ned could never understand, and as he had experienced a thousand times, twenty thousand times, they secured their bounty, and then were consumed by it.

Dragged for leagues across the surface of the world, the *Lincoln* had found its prey, and it was thoroughly outmatched. The monster flew under the deep, and their ship could only trot. Ned contained himself. When the professor fell overboard, and he saw that Farragut failed to notice, Ned threw himself into the infernal wake, amused that the professor's manservant Conseil had come to the same conclusion. Respect as he did such dedication, Ned considered his skills superior in such pursuit.

He chased them for hours. They never had a clue he was there. He shouted, his voice suffocated by the surf, and he considered their despair with a solemn heart. He began to wonder if he had underestimated the professor. He watched as the pair treaded water. This was a greater show of fortitude than he had afforded a fanatic. This, too, worried him. Its bitter reflection was certain to be worse.

This is the exact thought he had when he at last pulled alongside them, as they settled on the unlikeliest of perches: the hull of a vessel, a metal ship, the very object of their inquiry, the answer he had known all along. As strange men emerged from it and advanced upon them, Ned wanted to utter his confession, that he had conjured this devil just as much as any wild report, all the speculation that had driven the enlightened world crazy, until it at last settled at his doorstep, a ramshackle affair in a white-knuckle existence that had only ever felt natural in the circumstances that promised nothing but the constant pull of the unknown fate of adventurers.

And he prayed, not to a god, but to the family he thought for sure he was leaving behind forever...

THE YELLOW SUBMARINE, OR IN THE TOWN WHERE THEY WERE BORN

It is 1872. Pierre Aronnax marries Krystyna Ciszek. They have agreed to settle down in America, in the city of Woonsocket, Rhode Island, where French-Canadian immigrants have already been congregating to work in the mills, to escape from oppression in their home country. Pierre is a world-famous biologist. He has been convinced to come here not by the plight of these people who speak his native language, but by his new bride, who says she understands them better than he ever could.

It is 1890. Pierre is in his sixties, and yet Krystyna, who is the same age, by some miracle is still able to give birth to their son Mathurin, who, growing up among aging parents, cut off from extended family, knows little human warmth, and less of the strange circumstances that created him. He's impatient whenever Pierre makes the effort, pointing out the yellow submarine in the backyard of the house they've had built, renting out the second floor as a means to bring in money. When Mathurin leaves the home, he abandons both his parents and the submarine to ancient history.

It is 1912. Mathurin has himself married, to a woman named Oliva Gregoire, who convinces him to return home, Krystyna having died, leaving Pierre a widower, and although he agrees, Mathurin refuses to talk with his father. By this time he has forgotten all about the strange submarine rusting in the woods down the hill from the house. This same year Oliva gives birth to their son Jean, who as he grows up discovers the submarine and pesters Mathurin about it. To his embarrassment, Mathurin discovers that he has few answers, and in the meantime Pierre has passed away.

It is 1942. Jean and his wife Sarah have had a son of their own, Sylvio Aronnax. Jean has grown bitter about the submarine, and is angry when the growing Sylvio asks about it. They have a contentious relationship as Jean struggles to make a living. Like his father Mathurin, Jean had to work in the mills along with all the other French-speaking members of the community, and he resents it. Sylvio is enlisted into the military and serves a tour in the Vietnam War.

It is 1967. Sylvio marries Thursday Kim.

It is 1980. Julian Aronnax is born.

It is 1992. Thursday dies of cancer.

It is 1995. Julian conceives of the plan to resurrect the yellow submarine in his backyard. A classmate named Elle begins working with him on the project. At first he has no idea why, and then he doesn't care, and eventually it just seems natural. Elle's boyfriend helps out every now and then, a tacit reminder that there are no romantic prospects occurring here. They often work silently, although there are happy conversations and laughter, and frustration when they can't figure something out. Sylvio visits without comment a few times, and Elle asks Julian for some kind of explanation, but he proves equally reticent, until the day Sylvio picks up a ratchet and begins assisting them. Work continues apace, although the lengthy silences stretch still further and Elle finds herself crying with frustration. Sylvio still says nothing, walking off as if nothing at all has occurred, returning later with the family van and a trailer hitched to it, and they proceed with the laborious effort of transferring the submarine onto it, which is a task that feels impossible until finally Sylvio leaves again and returns with a friend who uses his truck to push the submarine upward and into its cradle.

It is now late in the year, and Julian and Elle have had many conversations about the frequent breaks Sylvio requires even when he's been doing something simple. He is dying, of course. Father and son never discuss this. They have secured access to a dock from which they will be able to attempt a launch of their unlikely expedition. Julian tells them to be patient with him, because he would like to say a few words about Pierre Aronnax, whose own journey aboard this vessel was even more unlikely and ended in disaster, of which Julian has finally found word in old editions of the Woonsocket Call.

There were conflicting reports. One claimed that the submarine was later discovered shipwrecked on a remote island, but this they know is impossible, since it has been sitting here in Woonsocket, forgotten by history, for a hundred years, a conversation that was avoided for generations of the Aronnax family.

Julian instead brings their attention to an article buried deep within the folds of a newspaper brittle and yellowed with age, an obituary for a man named Nemo, who settled in Woonsocket the same year as Pierre and Krystyna Aronnax. The notice explains that Nemo is a Polish expatriate, a political exile, and Krystyna's father. He fled, however, not from oppression, but his own activities, a campaign of terror across the world's oceans, against opponents of various nationalities, though none of them Russian, the people he had fought against in the January Uprising.

He pauses, and then asks them if this is a legacy worth continuing.

It is Sylvio who replies.

"It seems as if Nemo failed because of Pierre Aronnax. It seems as if we need to conclude this the same way it began."

Julian agrees. Elle agrees. Sylvio again departs to take a rest. The submarine has been sitting on the water for weeks. It has not been submerged yet. None of them is certain that it won't simply sink. Julian spends time in the library he's been restocking. Elle never visits him here, has never even stepped foot in it. It amazes Julian, how spacious it is in here, how anyone in the 1860s could have lived in here for months, years at a time, totally beyond the scope of what others achieved at the time with comparable technology. He should know; he's been reading up on it, and half the library aboard is dedicated to that history, a fitting tribute.

He sits in that library, alone, wishing Elle were there, wishing his father were. Wishing his mother was. If he quits now, he will already have succeeded beyond his wildest dreams. No one would even care. No one would even notice. That's something he learned through all of this, too. If he succeeded, if he spent a week cruising in this thing, what would it even prove? Elle would still leave his life, his father would still die. The name Aronnax would remain in obscurity. He's just a stupid kid, with just another stupid obsession. He's already achieved the impossible. That any of it happened already feels meaningless, even to him. Sometimes things happen, and it doesn't matter.

He hears something in the distance. He gets up, hears the sound ringing in the bowels of the submarine, and realizes it's his father, crying, who stops as soon as he realizes Julian is there.

"It's nothing. It's ridiculous. I was just singing, and then thought about your mother, and then the tears started, and I couldn't stop."

Julian has never heard his father be so forthright about anything. He can't even begin to process it. So he walks away again, leaving his father alone with his emotions. It feels like the right thing to do.

Later, Elle is standing beside Julian. His father is away, exhausted again, and he's struggling to decide if he should flip the switch. Julian wants to delay, wait for his father, let him have a choice, although Elle argues that it would be unfair to trap him underwater if he suddenly needed emergency attention...Julian agrees, reluctantly.

He flips the switch, and the yellow submarine begins its descent.

THE NAUTILUS, OR LIVED A MAN WHO SAILED THE SEA

"Her mother, Anna, was not the most beautiful woman I ever saw. Beautiful is something you admire. It is not something you fall in love with. You fall in love and see a different kind of beauty. The beauty becomes perfect in ways you did not previously imagine possible. It becomes estimable against beauty in ways other people would not be able to conceive, to see. That is the way of love. It sees the surface, of course, but in perception changes the surface to match the interior."

Fyodor listens to this and he knows his friend is speaking from the heart. They are on a hard journey, relieved only by the knowledge that they are taking a novel approach. Others travel by land, and that is surely worse, almost as bad as the desolate destination. They are confined aboard a dark vessel. They have little enough to eat, and no means to replenish their meager stock. They will run out of food before their circuitous route ends in Siberia. And no one will care. Some will die. That is the way of things.

"I met her during the war. Perhaps war is the best time to experience life. It is the only time we are truly honest with ourselves, the only time we can ignore the delusions we tell ourselves, and stare into the abyss of reality. I will not say that reality is grim. That is an interpretation, which can be good and can be bad, depending on our moods. But reality is reality. Although of course war is a perversion of reality, a marked effort to rewrite it."

Fyodor knows about writing. He has been called a great writer in his time, but it is also his writing that has condemned him to Siberia. There are people who will condemn you, on this earth, in this life, to fates worse than death for what you write, for what you think. They will not merely consider you an idiot, scoff at you, ridicule you; no, they will also persecute you, isolate you, make your life difficult in all manners of ways. And all this not because you hurt someone, but because you didn't think the right way.

"When I saw her I told myself then and there that this was the woman I was going to marry. I would move heaven and earth to convince her. Or I would trade a single night's passion. Whatever worked. And it did work. She gave birth to my daughter, and regardless of anything else that happened, I would always have my daughter. My daughter, whom I would watch grow up, either as participant in her life, or from afar. I would from that time define myself by someone else's life, someone else's achievements."

Fyodor wrote personal stories. That is what hurt the most about his fate. He did not write about the lives of others, but his own, and so when his work was condemned, he felt himself rejected all over again. Despite what some might tell you, a writer's life is almost entirely interior, and their work like his friend's beautiful woman. When someone rejects that, when they condemn you for it, if you are a true writer, it is a pure act of betrayal, worse than any other kind.

"When the war began, I was a conscript in the Russian army, same as so many other Polishmen. I was just another soldier. Of course, soldiers talk. Especially among the Polishmen, which the Russians were foolish enough to let intermingle, and in fact ensured were the only voices we heard, asked to obey but to listen only to the voice of resistance, of bitter disappointment with a world devoid of self-determination, a country that was not ours. Amongst our own kind, what else would we speak of?"

What else indeed? Fyodor wrote only of his experiences because it was the only thing he knew to be true. Life in this century was constant turmoil. Revolution behind it and certain revolution ahead, across the entire globe, empires large and small exceeding their grasp, no longer certain of their place in the world, realizing in great frustration that they would have to ally themselves with other nations or risk annihilation. The individual, the smallest most pitiable history had yet seen, a murderer equal to an orphan, unprecedented, unparalleled, treated utterly without remorse, celebrated and then once more rejected. Cast out to the hinterlands. Survive in the wilds, ye who have been cast out from paradise!

"This very vessel, the Nautilus, a revolutionary maritime phenomenon, the backdrop of my first glimpse of her. Together with my mariner cavalry, anonymous, I saw my Anna scrubbing uselessly, projecting the false promise of a nation that would inherit the world, one iron way or another, scuttling off as we boarded. I stole away, separated from the pack, and enjoyed my last night of freedom, and she whispered in my ear, 'It doesn't have to be the last.' She knew all about me, she said, what we were planning to do, and that she had prepared the way, stashed among the nooks and crannies of our coffin the means to accomplish it. That is precisely how this journey began."

The January Uprising began after the American Civil War did, and ended before it did. It was the campaign as Americans on both sides of that conflict had imagined theirs would be, short, brutal, decisive. Total failure. I wrote in chronicle of it, a tale of a family caught between god and country. This was what condemned me. God had no place in a story about country, in which the country *was* god.

"The Russian officers never saw it coming. We slaughtered them all. We would have won, too, had any of us known the first thing about operating the Nautilus."

Fyodor and his friend Nemo repeated history, except this time Nemo had learned. He had become master of the Nautilus. The only casualty Nemo regretted this time was Fyodor's, his friend, who drowned. Later, as he cast about pity, he found a manuscript his friend had left behind, about a great friendship, something entirely inconsistent with the work the writer had previously tackled. He howled at the loss all over again.

He pointed his ship away from Siberia. He forgot the Russians entirely. He set about his targets the ships of the French, the Ottomans, the British, Sardinians, all those who had allied themselves against the Russians, before, in the last of the crusades, and then forgotten his people when they needed them most. His reign of terror was holy vengeance.

And then of course one day he was at last discovered, by a Frenchman, of all people, who sought only to learn what this was all about. And what indeed to do with such a man?

PEPPER, OR A VIEW FROM THE FUTURE

It is 2233. More than two hundred years have passed. A woman named Pepper, speaking an English that would be difficult for you to comprehend, although not impossible, a dialect that might sound like it comes from a foreign country, as indeed it would, for the future, as elusive as it always seems to be, is as foreign a language as the past, no matter how much we love to guess about it. And we will always be wrong. The future, as it is experienced by those living it, is indistinguishable from our present. It is exactly the same. Except, a little different. It is natural to assume the difference would be radical, but it is not. It never is. It is mostly cosmetic.

Which is why the submarine Nautilus exists in 2233 just as surely as it does in 2021, 1995, 1863. It is a vessel that contains dreams, in equal measure, as with all things, with nightmares.

This woman named Pepper never heard of a man called Nemo. She never heard anything about Pierre Aronnax, Julian, Elle, any of them. But she knows all about the Nautilus, although for her it is not a submarine at all, but a spaceship! It remains hauntingly adaptable, alas.

How it came to this state is immaterial, except that it happened and Pepper had nothing at all to do with it, something that occurred as distant from her time as Pierre's is from Julian's. Pepper interests us as the operator, in 2233, of the Nautilus, yes, but also for the fateful journey she herself takes aboard it.

She of course found it in a scrapyard, having once more fallen into a state of detritus, the object worthy of a thousand museums once more neglected. (We believe that history, and memory, records all useful things, but this would be a fallacy.) For Pepper, here was not the task of reviving it, rebuilding, repurposing. She saw it for what it was, and for her it was a ticket to the moon.

Now, in 2233 there are a great many people living on the moon, which then has a new name, although the context for it would be a considerable digression from this tale, so we will not bother further with that line of inquiry at this time. Pepper's interest in this pursuit was not to flee a dying planet, in case you were worried, not the establishment of a habitable moon necessitated by such a development.

As with all migrations, and all mountains, it was undertaken because it was there.

Pepper, by the way, is 31, if that interests you, informs you of her basic character. She is just shy of five feet, five inches, has tan skin, dark curly hair, and when she smiles she has a delightful set of dimples, although anyone who knows her will sadly inform you that you won't get to see them as often as you'd like.

She is not routinely employed, and when she is it is a host of occupations you will find yourself sifting through, all of them, like the moon, like mountains, because they were there. She has a degree in anthropology, a professor with a British accent once having inadvertently wooed her into that field, but no actual fields, unfortunately, Pepper having no motivation to find employment with that credential.

And she does not have a boyfriend, no husbands in her past, and no children. What awaits her is her nephew. Her brother is a single parent, and sent Pepper a transmission requesting temporary assistance. She didn't think twice about it; she has good history with her brother and her nephew is only recently born, and she already adores him far beyond what she previously thought possible.

So she went digging in a scrapyard, and there it was. Destined to, at last, become reduced to meaningless slabs of metal, no more to roam. Pepper was not an aficionado of spaceships, as you reading this now assume that of course she would have to be, living in the future as she does. To be fair, even in your time not everyone has or wants a car. It is exactly like that.

The Nautilus, at this point in its existence, has the advantage of automated systems. All Pepper has to do is switch it on. Of course, at its advanced age and state of disrepair, it doesn't turn on automatically, and not for several days. She buys it anyway, for cheap, practically for nothing! She has it delivered. She lives in an apartment, and she has a docking port she has never previously used.

Going to work during this brief span is interminable. She is in fact quitting this job to accept this sudden responsibility way off on the moon. She hated the job anyway. She has no idea what happens after this moon thing, but that's something to worry about later.

She keeps fiddling with the Nautilus. She knows a thing or two. A stray cat who always comes to her doorstep for something to eat has snuck its way inside the ship. Pepper doesn't mind. She mentally adds tins of cat food to the meager list of items she'll be taking with her. The cat nudges her. She reconsiders for the hundredth time something she's already tried. And persistence, and a little cat, pays off. The Nautilus roars to life!

She leaves it running, paranoid, and dashes into her apartment to grab her suitcases. The cat is purring in the pilot's seat, and Pepper gently nudges it out of her way as she settles in, punching in the coordinates for her brother's place on the moon.

She feels gravity digging into her as the Nautilus ascends, breaking orbit and shooting out into the vacuum of space, surrounded suddenly by total darkness. She finds the Earth gleaming with sunlight, as with all things in the night sky, when she glimpses backward, the cat stretching out in her lap. Funny, that cat never let Pepper come near her before, except to set the tin down in front of it. The cat would dart if she ever dared touch it.

The Nautilus is indeed ancient. The trip would have taken minutes in a new model, but Pepper doesn't mind. She unbuckles and heads to its library, which she stocked with the bulk of what she took from her apartment. She has a wide assortment, antiquated by nearly all standards, of physical titles, all of them classics. Though even in 2233 it's a chore for readers to get through, Pepper always adored the one about the whale, and she has an unbelievable number of variations on the Trojan War, which has fascinated her since high school. She has plenty of time to have another look.

Pepper has never previously been to space. There's a port in the library that increasingly distracts her. There's still nothing much to see, and everything. There's the moon, looming ever larger. She loves the feeling of being totally eclipsed by this void, a tiny speck in a sea that stretches widely, as life can sometimes conspire to obscure, humanity so often bent on filling such things, and then lamenting their loss, with no loss of irony.

Even the docking procedures are automated. Her brother, and her nephew, are waiting. Pepper darts in the direction of her nephew, Sam, and apologizes to her brother, while making googly faces.

She sits next to Sam in the transport her brother drives into the city.

"I saw your ship," her brother says. "You have no idea where it came from, do you?"

"Of course I do!" Pepper says. "It came from a junk heap."

"Before that," her brother says.

"There is literally nothing before this moment," Pepper says, staring at Sam, who is napping.

"You really have no idea," her brother says.

"Could not care less," Pepper says.

"Do you even know what its name is?" her brother says.

"How dare you call your baby an 'it,' and forget his name!" Pepper says. "It's Sam. Your baby's name is Sam."

"The ship, Pepper," her brother says.

"I think it said 'Nautilus' on the dashboard," Pepper says. " The manufacturer, probably."

"Please never change," her brother says. "Listen, I'm going to be visiting the past. That's why you're here, Pepper. To watch Sam while I go visit the past. There's something I need to see. The permit was easy to get. Nobody in that office saw the significance, anymore than you did, when you found that ship. I can't help but think it's fate, although I guess it was kind of inevitable, where we grew up and all. Maybe I knew you were going to find it. All the pieces are coming together, Pepper."

Pepper didn't catch all of that. Sam woke up. Sam started crying, and Pepper, to her utter astonishment, somehow knew how to help it stop. All she knows is that for the next few months, Sam is going to be her entire world. And she's already convinced she'll do anything to make it last forever.

She can't stop smiling, her dimples deep as canyons...

NEMO, OR HE HAS ALL HE NEEDS

"I congratulate you. And now, I must also impress on you the fact that you will spend the rest of your life as my guest."

Pierre, Ned and Conseil had no sooner discovered the truth of the monster they had sought than realized the monster was of an entirely different kind than they could possibly have imagined.

Ned's first and only thought was escape. If there was anything else, it was the belief that he needed to end this thing in exactly the manner he had made his life's work. He would have to kill Nemo.

Conseil had no thought except what he had pledged his life to as well.

And as ever, Pierre Aronnax yearned to know more.

I will not recount for you here the conversations he and Nemo shared, the extent to which Nemo sought to justify himself, if he made any effort at all. In fact, he was far more interested in impressing Pierre with what he had created, giving a tour of his vessel, its exact operations, and even the very ocean floor, as very few living souls had to that point in history managed to accomplish.

He never once uttered the name of the man he hated most in this world, the name of the ship which even then was in the same pursuit as Farragut, aboard the *Lincoln*, maintained. That was a private affair. It was in fact Nemo's whole story; not the manner in which he had obtained the Nautilus, the motivation to do so, or the campaign of terror that mystified a planet, no one daring imagine the identity of the thing that had wrecked so many ships with such malice.

The idea of becoming prisoner to such a maniac didn't even occur to Pierre. As with all his pursuits he got caught up in the romance of it. No protest from Ned, no suggestion of a look from Conseil bothered him.

Nemo was above all else charismatic. He was a brilliant host. Aside from the notion that tragedy could never leave, and thus reveal the truth of the monster, end his campaign, he gave them every liberty, and they found the Nautilus spacious, and a graceful navigator of the sea. Even Ned had to admit he had never before experienced such an effortless traversing.

They peered out the ports and saw nothing but the earth's waters about, marine life passing by as if their presence were natural. Ned spotted whales, and his hand twitched, and Pierre patted it. They were utterly dwarfed. The whales passed by.

It was when the octopus approached that Nemo gave pause. He made no mention of it, but his face turned pale, and he could be seen to shudder. Ned laughed to see it, Pierre scowled at him.

The octopus advanced, its tangled limbs brushing brazenly against the hull of the Nautilus. Pierre thought that would be it, but Nemo began shouting a series of orders to his crew, none of which Pierre could follow, and he had witnessed many such scenes over the years.

The limbs began pounding, and the orders began to sound more desperate.

Then they began clutching the hull.

One covered the port Pierre had been viewing it from, obscuring his view completely. He began to grow nervous. Nemo had vanished, and all the crew with him, busy at stations his guests could not access from their quarters, where they had decided to settle.

Again Ned's hand twitched. It was almost visible, his absent harpoon, confiscated from him when they had been taken aboard, its contours exactly matching the space he left in his palm. Conseil stood absently. Pierre wanted only to know what course of action Nemo would take.

"We should make our escape," Ned said. "We will have no better prospects than these."

"Into the embrace of the cephalopod," Conseil said.

"Better to take our chances," Ned said.

The puckers revealed, briefly, a figure out in the sea, in one of the containment suits they had used to brave the crushing pressures of the deep. Pierre knew it was Nemo. He saw without needing to try the deep desperation in the man's face.

He knew this had happened at all because they had created an unexpected disruption to the life of the Nautilus.

Nemo held Ned Land's harpoon. Pierre had seen that much. The octopus was massive in scale, wrapped around the whole of the vessel, large as it had seemed inside when they took their tour, marveled at Nemo's library, a depository of knowledge from a world its collector had rejected utterly, convinced that he had been forsaken. Pierre found himself worrying about those books now. Not exactly Alexandria, but that was what flashed through his mind, irrationally.

He envisioned the struggle playing out. Peaceful as Nemo appeared in repose, Pierre saw in every particular the man capable of what he had done, and the challenge now before him. Roused, he was an animal, all brutal instinct. Nothing but. Nothing human...

When the tentacle dropped, Pierre was sure, at first, that Nemo had lost. Then he saw inky waters bubbling with crimson, and he knew.

He greeted Nemo at the hatch and demanded they go to port.

"That is both a simple and difficult request," Nemo said. "Nautilus is crippled. She won't survive my intentions."

It was that exact moment his foe appeared. Not Farragut, not the *Lincoln*, but Nemo's unnamed nemesis. Nautilus had been forced to surface, and it was what Nemo had been trying to avoid for years.

Russian, surely.

The cannon struck like thunder. Nemo at once demanded Nautilus to descend again, but in doing so he guaranteed its fate. Compromised, its only course was to follow Pierre's advice.

When it reached New England shores, the *Lincoln* was there to greet Nautilus. Farragut perched at the hatch as Pierre, Conseil, Ned, Nemo and all his men emerged. He was magnanimous. He pressed no further charges or terms, except that Nemo endure the rest of his days in defeat, exile, an utter failure, perhaps to share his secrets with the American military, but that was all.

The Nautilus passed into history, crippled, beyond repair, a relic ahead of its time, but now a part of that time, advanced at one time, but then only a thing of the past. So much flotsam.

Conseil returned to Europe, Ned Land to Nantucket, and then to whaling. Pierre and Nemo settled in Woonsocket. Nemo aged rapidly, a defeated, broken man who spoke to no one, forgetting even that spectacular library, no longer seeing much use in it, or the mind that had created it.

Pierre Aronnax kept as treasure the harpoon that had ushered the end of a world. Then he met the love of his life.

KRYSTYNA, OR A FAMILY MATTER

Pierre never could keep a secret from her.

He told her all the stories he'd heard about her
mother, from Nemo, all the stories about the war.

Lies, she told him. All of it, lies.

They would sit in outdoor cafes, after his lectures,
"Very European," she would tease him, with
sadness in her eyes, and he would tell her
everything.

They had met in one of them. She had just arrived
in America, and knew only Polish, and he heard her
struggling with the waiter, and he offered to help.
He knew dozens of languages, he said, and he
bought her coffee that day. The next time she
bought coffee for both of them.

"I was ashamed," she later admitted. "I knew so little."

He always suspected she spent so much time with the immigrants so she could hide among them. He never dared say this to her. She learned French, she learned English. She stopped speaking Polish, but never stopped dreaming of home. She saved all her money so she could go back, to visit. Never to live there again. It had become a foreign country.

He never told her, but when the day came, he thought he was losing her forever. She was going alone, and he was convinced he would never see her again. He felt strangely giddy, and stupid, and in another lifetime he would have been right. She was gone the whole summer, and then she was back in Woonsocket, and they married in a private ceremony, and posed for pictures that in later years looked truly as if they came from another world, pictures Julian Aronnax would stare at in wonder...

She would go to church every Sunday, with Pierre at her side. On those days it was still the Latin mass, a language no one in attendance knew, except perhaps the priest. She knew the words but not what they meant. That was prayer to her. The parishioners were family to her. That was what the faith meant. It was almost her entire life.

When Mathurin was born, life changed utterly all over again. Pierre sought to distance them from the past. They were old, a kind of miracle, when these things were still possible. She wanted Mathurin to know everything.

She wanted him to know all about Nemo. Nemo, who had been her father...

Nemo abandoned her mother to fight his war. There was no way around this fact. That is what he chose to do. Anna was a schoolgirl, an idealist, who believed in the fight before Nemo did, who lectured him every day for what felt like an eternity until he found himself caught up in it himself, drafted by the Russians to fight his own people. Anna told him to resist, to run away with her, but he didn't. He cooperated, and only after that changed his mind.

She never forgave him.

She bore his child, gave birth, never saw him again.

She was abandoned.

When the reports started coming in about the Nautilus, she observed coldly. She didn't dare to believe that it was Nemo until she couldn't believe anything else. A fanatic is born out of first rejecting the idea. Then she heard more, and she knew, she was certain.

The evolution of the Nautilus was a long one. At first a battleship, and then a prisoner transport, and then cast into the hands of the rebellion, in Poland it was famous, in Russia infamous. She kept news clippings for years about it. She could trace its whole history.

And then it was *lost* to history. It vanished from the face of the earth, no longer surfacing even for an instant.

She found it in other reports. She followed the reports of dockworkers. She followed reports of the war. She followed the reports of deserters. She followed the reports of survivors.

The whole story played out as her daughter grew up, became a woman, before the uprising, before the war, its abrupt termination, failure, and as reports of a different kind entirely began to surface.

Anna named her daughter Krystyna.

And Krystyna kept all this alive in her heart, and told it to Mathurin.

Mathurin, who grew up hating his father, who grew old believing himself a failure, who couldn't stop Nemo's campaign before it ended in tragedy.

But the whole *thing* had been tragedy...

How to explain such things? She did her best, but sometimes, a son doesn't care, no matter how much she loves him, no matter how much she gives him, what a mother does, because he yearns after his father, knows what he hasn't gotten, what he has been denied, what has been lost.

She recognizes this. It eats away at her, even more than her aging body. Some grow old quickly, some in slow motion. If she had lived long enough, she would have hardly have looked different at ninety as she had at eighty. Some look and feel seventy when they are sixty. I don't know if it's a choice or consequence. I wouldn't trust those who tell you which, personally.

She is alive when Mathurin marries, when he gives birth. The day his father died, Mathurin's interest in his own past dies, and his mother stops trying. She stops speaking, two generations of her family silenced, and their history lost.

But she keeps a diary.

She writes all this down. She has flowery penmanship. It can be difficult to read. Yet the diary remains with the family, in the basement of the home the family maintains throughout the century.

It remains undiscovered for decades. One day Julian, always restless, always searching, always yearning, discovers it. He remembers the grave they visit, how no one can tell him much about this woman, how she died.

He spends weeks trying to decipher it. Sometimes he forgets all about it. He could never keep a journal. He decides to try again.

One day, he's reading something else, and his mind wanders. He has his breakthrough, realizing that all that time with the diary wasn't wasted at all, like the words to a song that suddenly cross his lips despite never having tried singing it before.

He returns to it. And he learns.

And he decides to do something about it. Then and there, in 1995, his father dying, his mother already dead, his family ending, his future in doubt...Julian Aronnax resolves to do the impossible. He is far too young. He doesn't know anything about the world.

He does not yet know that all stories are circular, if you understand them...

SYLVIO, OR AN ARONNAX STORY

I went into remission.

I went into remission after...

Is it possible to call yourself an intelligent being if
you have no idea the effect you have on the lives of
the people around you? I'm not talking sociopaths.
I'm talking regular people. Sometimes I think Hell
is filled with them. Sometimes I think the greatest,
and only real, sin is a willfully oblivious life.

This can happen for any number of perfectly
innocent reasons. It might be a defensive
mechanism. In fact, in probably every instance
that's exactly what it is. But the mark of an
intelligent being, surely, is the ability to rise above

circumstances. There are some circumstances for which this is impossible. But most of them aren't. Ignorance, in the face of alternatives, is a choice.

I made a choice, a long time ago, to live a selfish life. Most of the time I had no idea I was even doing it. Routine becomes habit, becomes nature. It began before I could even retain long term memory. When I was a boy. Before I was even born. Inheritance can be deadly.

It doesn't matter that a hundred years ago I had an ancestor who was brilliant, who changed the world, saved it, without anyone knowing it ever happened. He ruined a family in the process. It's that simple. (Do I condemn him or thank him? Sometimes, maybe always, the answers aren't that simple.)

I grew up in a home that didn't really know what to do with small children, and I was the youngest of a large family, and no one ever let me forget it. With my siblings, it was constant resentment. With my parents, it was as if I never, ever grew up. No one wants to live like that. Then again, until you have the courage, or luck, to change your circumstances, you're hardly in a position to argue the point.

I idolized my older brothers. I saw them becoming men. I wanted to do everything they could do, and that was the scope of my imagination. Other people had heroes in the real world. Mine existed in a pressure cooker.

And by the time I left the house, I had been the last one there for years. My oldest brother could have been my father. Alienation was a family tradition.

It was my son who saved me, and I spent fifteen years fighting it. But, which I say with the faintest, most damning praise, it finally happened.

I had tried to be a good father, I really had, but I could see it without any effort, that Julian had no warmth in his heart for me, which he considered to be a reflection. He was the model only of my anger.

When the diagnosis happened, I hoped in vain that it might thaw our relationship, but I could see, too, how hopeless that was, because I had done nothing but shared a medical fact with him. It was just the same as if I had told him about a hangnail. And I saw him drift further.

He was, instead, becoming obsessed, and for too long I couldn't fathom why or what could possibly be so interesting (I had of course never bothered to acquaint myself with his interior life, as I never had with anyone else, for that matter; we think such things are impossible, and by "we" I mean those of us as I discussed at the start of this, we monsters). He told me a brief account of Pierre Aronnax, omitting any mention of the name Nemo. He told it to me in a dismissive fashion, because he knew I wasn't really interested.

Later, when I was feeling sorry for myself, after a treatment, I began thinking about this Pierre

Aronnax, a very vague memory struggling to the surface. My father, when I had been very young, had mentioned this man, too. I couldn't remember what I had heard. And so I asked my son.

"Tell me more," I said.

Of course this is a lie. I didn't do any such thing.

I instead watched him from a distance. I watched the girl become interested in this thing before I did. I knew they weren't in a relationship. My son was not the sort to pursue such things. Of course I discouraged it. What else would I do? And besides, he was already a solitary sort. Of course he would be. And so what other possibility? This girl, Elle...

I had no choice, as far as I was concerned. I began helping in silence. I had finally had an inkling of the truth, an epiphany, a thunderbolt. Instead of going blind, I found I could now see, that I *had* been blind...

Of course I was growing weaker all this time. My son knew, and we never talked about it, but as these events progressed I saw his heart thawing. I don't know if it was too late for mine, if there was anything I could do, in one lifetime, in a hundred, to make up for the cannon that had been forged. To finally end this fruitless war, and still have some good come from it.

I was at my weakest when they got the thing in the water. Assisting in that was the last thing I did to help. I sat on the dock, collapsed, waving them off, telling them I was fine, go off and do it already! when I knew, with absolutely certainty, that this would end only one way.

And it took no time at all for that conclusion to happen.

The damn thing sank immediately. That's how it seemed, anyway. I know they were in there tinkering, whatever, but in my mind's eye one minute I was getting the thing in the water and the next I was diving in, no strength, no strength, I couldn't believe I was doing it, and pulling my son, struggling hard against me, crying great gasps of tears, his mouth filling over and over again with water, and...

That was how quickly she died. That was how we repaid her. Was there ever a suggestion she lived happily thereafter? That they drifted apart?

And there in front of me, my son was drowning on dry land. I had gotten him out of the water, but it was still in his lungs, and I had no more power in me. I had used all the unknown reserves already, and there was no one around to help. This was before cellular phones. His eyes were bulging, his skin growing tight, his mouth seizing. My son.

I threw my hand into the air. I hammered it down. I did this, and I felt no power in me. I did it again. I could hear a howling sound, unearthly, unnatural. All this time I thought of the man he should have become, of the hard lessons he had had to learn, the incredible thing he had accomplished, with all but no help from me...

I told myself, stop with this self-pity! This is not about you! This was never about you!

And he lay there on the dock, and my pitiful efforts were ineffective, and...

For the briefest of moments, I thought I had done it. I thought I had done the impossible. I thought there had been a miracle.

He coughed once.

And then he was gone.

And for a very long time, all was lost.

Later, as I lay in a hospital bed, someone explained to me that we had been found. It was too late for my son, but not for me, and I found no solace in that, none in the announcement, later, of my remission.

I shut myself away again. Having learned nothing at all, even when I had lost everything. Not everyone is Job. But that's not something they tell you. But maybe they should.

Then one day a man came to visit. He said his name was Jimmy. He said he had gone to school with my son. He told me he had never thought much of Julian (and I wanted to cry), and in fact had forgotten all about him until one day the most incredible of coincidences, maybe, and maybe he made the whole thing up, maybe he'd seen something in an old paper, about what happened, and it jogged his memory, and the best he could admit to was a lie.

Anyway, he told me that he *did* remember my son, and, as a new father (I suspect not *that* new), he found himself rethinking *his* childhood, about the people he'd wished had been in it, and then he realized, Julian *had* been in it. And he had taken him for granted.

And maybe things worked out the way they did and there was no way to change that now. He in fact pulled out a newspaper clipping, about my son, about what happened, and he asked me if the thing was still at the bottom of the river. I told him that as far as I knew, it was. And I wanted it to stay there.

He wasn't happy with that reply. He said it was worth exploring. And without saying anything, with no visible display that something had happened, I had my breakthrough, the real one, the one I had been working on since my boy started his project all those years earlier...

I still had a chance.

And, I suppose, that's the whole point.

POSTSCRIPT

The origin of this story was a separate project, an attempt to present the classic Jules Verne novel *Twenty Thousand Leagues Under the Sea* only up to the point before Captain Nemo enters the narrative. I had taken the trouble of transcribing the text and preparing a document for publication through Amazon's Kindle platform, which rejected it on the basis of an absence of a translator's note (Verne being French, he wrote his story in that language, of course), something that hadn't occurred to me. No doubt had I pursued the project through some official channel this wouldn't have been a problem, but no recourse I decided instead to walk away. The particulars as to why I was interested in the project are explained separately, but for now let's talk about *Aronnax* itself.

In a lot of ways, this is a story about heritage. The character of Sylvio Aronnax was based first on my uncle and godfather, Gerry Laramee, until I drifted in the direction of my father (Sylvio in fact being his middle name). I have for years been interested in exploring my family tree in general, which was where that element came from, although here it's a rough sketch and I have a very different story I want to write about my grandfather, Romeo Laramee, previously touched upon in a short story entitled "Hold Me Not, Let Me Go," published in the collection *Nazi Crimes*.

Aronnax was written when Kindle introduced its Vella program, a venue for serialized fiction, I'm certain intended for material not at all similar to what I ended up writing (even less so *Nine Panel Grid*, which I wrote later and published as a book before *Aronnax*), probably much more like the stuff you'll find at, say, Wattpad, the would-be popular, genre material they've been peddling to young readers in recent decades.

I've got to confess I have no idea how breaking into publishing works when you *aren't* pursuing that, or working through literary journals, workshops, if you're foolish enough to think your writing is good and you simply write in your spare time…I know readers have certain expectations that I don't typically feel interested in fulfilling, such as filling in narrative with descriptive elements, which is why I eventually drifted in the direction of first person narration, so that the focus is on interior reflection rather than exterior exposition, and have been developing this for years, hoping to find material that would interest general readers and, hopefully, publishers.

Aronnax is, among other things, an effort to find that material, and yes, to reclaim a story that I thought had real potential, a familiar one, and yet something that had not truly been appreciated for what it was. What follows is more on how that came to be, as well as a timeline of the mysterious events leading up to first contact with the elusive Captain Nemo.

The story I ended up writing *does* include Nemo, but a reclaimed Nemo, the one Verne originally intended to feature, which I thought was more interesting, the one entangled in real history, even while Verne's own Nemo ended up being sensational, untethered from the real world. I don't know if obscuring Nemo's origins affected the story Verne would have written anyway, or if an important detail was simply lost; I still find the Nemo material in Verne's work inferior to the elements preceding it, not really worthy of conversation with other classic works of that era, and perhaps why the book itself is better known for its title and the *character* of Nemo than for its content, much less story (even those who have never read, for example, *Strange Case of Dr Jeckyll and Mr Hyde*, would be able to tell you its basic plot, or *The Portrait of Dorian Gray*, or *Moby-Dick*, where anyone roughly informed could tell you about Ahab and his whale; no such common knowledge exists for our Nemo).

Once again, shifting the focus definitively to Pierre Aronnax proved unavoidable to me…

NEMO WITHOUT NEMO

So, the audacity of stating *Twenty Thousand Leagues Under the Sea* is better…without Captain Nemo.

I had never read the book before downloading a copy onto an ereader in 2016. I walked around Hampton, Virginia, reading it, and perhaps as you may know, the Pokémon Go craze had just begun, so among my early impressions of the book was in fact being asked by a passing motorist if I were playing the game, capturing the digital pocket monsters, to which I responded, No, I'm reading a book!

I found myself quite engrossed in it (the book, not
the game!), a certain kind of revelatory experience,
as I knew the title and the idea that Captain Nemo
was involved somehow far more than anything to
do with its plot.   What I discovered was something
very much akin to what I *did* know pretty well: the
seafaring literature of Herman Melville, including
the much-lauded, and rightfully so, *Moby-Dick*,
which is just as famously difficult to appreciate as it
seems to meander along whatever topics, including
an in-depth study on the art of whaling itself, that
Melville happened to find interesting, which at the
time much alienated critics and readers, and left him
in very sorry literary peril (somehow!).

The whole of the opening act of *Twenty Thousand
Leagues*, in fact, does not feature Nemo at all! It
instead features a Frenchman named Aronnax,
which is why I have named this version in his
honor.

By the time the book *does* reach Nemo, or so I
determined, my interest ground to a halt. I found it
plauding, unengaging, meandering, in all the wrong
ways, Nemo guiding the trio of adventurers who
had inadvertently sought him along pedestrian
episodes as they puzzle out what exactly they've
gotten themselves into.

In fact, I never finished reading it. This is not
something you would expect to read in a scholarly
effort of any kind. Probably such an admission
would be turned away from reputable publishers,

but since I currently ply my trade in self-publication, I don't have that problem. I'm free to do what I want!

I intended to! That was five years ago, and while I had the physical copy of the book turned out for years, I never got around to it. Part of why I had it sticking out was because I had this project itself in mind, and the intention to try and work around the Nemo problem, to capture the whole book, even with less radical editing, to even still include Nemo himself!

You can see that I reconsidered that. This is a version of *Twenty Thousand Leagues* without its most famous character, the reason anyone even knows it exists, without Captain Nemo!

So, why? Because I believe given the chance at a new context, it can be rediscovered. I don't think it's a radical suggestion to say Verne did not end up creating an enduring classic endlessly and enthusiastically reread and rediscovered. There is no great tradition here as there is for other works of the 19th century, such as *Dracula, Frankenstein, Pride & Prejudice*. Hollywood doesn't endlessly retell the story of Captain Nemo. The only significant cinematic depiction I can think of (and I am relatively well-informed on the subject) is his inclusion in *League of Extraordinary Gentlemen*, the adaptation of the Alan Moore comic that nobody much takes seriously, but I like anyway. In the movie, Nemo is nothing much more than a host as his famous ship the Nautilus transports the erstwhile superhero team along their escapades.

Every classic literary character in that story, at least the movie version, has some kind of arc, except Nemo.

The story of Nemo goes, in case you're wondering, in case, like me, you never finished reading the book (yet), is that he forsook the world and went about his voyages on a wild course of revenge.

But Captain Ahab he is not! In fact, half the reason I sought to recapture the story, without him, is that the opening act is such a great snapshot of the era succeeding Melville's obsessed whaler, a segue into the world we would recognize, the wider world of the 20th century. It's less about the answer and more about the mystery.

And that's a totally different story, because the answer is Nemo, and the mystery really has nothing at all to do with him. Aronnax and his companions set out to solve the mystery the whole world wants to know of what has been causing shipwrecks and general sea mayhem. Everyone thinks it's a genuine sea creature of previously unknown dimensions. The 19th century gave us dinosaurs, after all, so anything was possible. Here in the 21st century we still linger on undiscovered creatures like the Loch Ness Monster and Big Foot, convinced they're more than legend, just waiting to be catalogued in the official annals of the animal kingdom. We did in fact find many alien beings in the deepest parts of the world's oceans, though none of them remotely capable of the carnage Aronnax finds so compelling.

Particularly coming off the COVID-19 pandemic, the way in which the world debates and responds to the mystery in *Twenty Thousand Leagues* seemed itself all the more relevant. There was an intense need to conform to the emergency of the pandemic, which itself was the only responsible thing to do, but in effect it silenced all conversation, negated all other reactions as wrong. The world Jules Verne depicts in his fictional emergency is quite different. Aronnax himself, something of an expert, comes to a conventional conclusion, which having reached it helps justify as the expectation of the answer from most authorities, but respects Ned Land, the harpooner, to have his own opinions, as they discuss matters aboard the vessel carrying them to their destiny. The third member of the trio we end with is Conseil, Aronnax's faithful servant, a stock figure that has somewhat vanished in recent years. Conseil (pronounced "con-say," which in 2016 I hadn't yet confirmed, so at times I pronounced to myself as "council," as "conceal" didn't sound dignified enough, and that was my default) is a name derived from a French word meaning "advice," making the character doubly ironic for modern readers. Yet Conseil is Aronnax's best and first ally when he really needs one, after he's tossed overboard late in the act and lost at sea; Conseil thinks nothing of following after him, even if neither has anymore proven chances of survival (they are in turn saved by Ned, and then by the answer to the mystery, which is of course the Nautilus, which is of course Captain Nemo's submarine).

Part of what attracted me to Aronnax as a lead character is my Franco-American heritage, which has its roots in Canada and of course France itself, distant enough in my generation to be an unfortunate mystery of its own. Aronnax, then, is a surrogate figure, and Verne, being himself French (as I type these words I live in Tampa, Florida, which has a Jules Verne park).

Aronnax is immersed in a full understanding of the global community around him. The vessel he, Conseil and Ned head out aboard is American. At the time I was struggling through *Twenty Thousand Leagues* I also read a book by Teddy Roosevelt in which he laments Woodrow Wilson's apparent lack of awareness that such an interconnected world was in existence. He was of course attempting to get elected president again at the time, and he and Wilson had very much opposite views on everything. Wilson is best remembered today as the originator of the League of Nations idea, but to hear Roosevelt is to view it as a repeat of a performance that had already failed in the 19th century in fruitless peace conferences.

And, well, whatever your views on any of that, you can begin to see the context from which Verne imagined his story, in fact the story he was really trying to tell, perhaps a warning of the very environment that ended up producing two world wars. I am not a scholar of Jules Verne. He died in 1905. A contemporary of his, L. Frank Baum, the writer of the Oz books, *was* very much interested in all of this, and infused his thoughts in his fantastical landscape (far more allegory than many fans today might suspect; even Teddy Roosevelt pops up!). So I don't think it's hard to at least imagine the possibility. What else is the genre of science fiction about?

Keeping Aronnax as the lead character of the story, then, as he is in the opening act anyway (even at the point I leave off from, Nemo is still a few chapters away!), refocuses the whole thing, at least in this form, into an exploration of the mystery itself, and Verne's version of the classic sea narrative that had once served the likes of Melville so well. (Like fans of car racing, anticipating crashes, readers were actually more interested in the spectacular disasters awaiting such voyagers, and the cannibals that might be encountered, which is something Melville himself experienced, and made his name writing about.)

So why end without having actually reached Nemo? Why end with the mystery mostly intact?

Well, blame *Lost*. The TV series that debuted in 2004 and ended in 2010 was for much of its run wildly popular. Its every decision was viewed as genius. It could even get away with making blatant literary allusions, often merely by displaying the books themselves as props or references. Desmond, for instance, read every Dickens except *Our Mutual Friend* (if you've read it, you can probably see the significance to the character), so he could say he had one more left.

Suffice to say, I was and remain a big fan. I followed along eagerly for all six seasons. I gobbled it up. I thought it was the television equivalent of a literary classic, the closest anything in the medium has come to such a status. It had every wild ambition, and leaned into all of it.

Every season turned on a new revelation. At the end of the first season the characters have blown open a mysterious hatch. Viewers speculated endlessly, as they did every aspect (and they ended up spoiling it for themselves in the process, because once you're only satisfied with your guesses, the answers can't possibly satisfy), and of course in the second season we find out the truth, which leads to other things, after other things, and…

I decided to end my version of *Twenty Thousand Leagues* on exactly that note. The discovery of the existence of the Nautilus, though having no clue what it actually is, much less who lives inside of it, is very much like blowing open that hatch. If you were a fan of *Lost* who *didn't* think the Dharma Initiative, much less Desmond, was good enough, because it didn't itself solve the riddle of the mysterious island (that's where fans made the connection with Jules Verne, which also happens to be the book where Captain Nemo's adventures conclude), then you might appreciate this decision.

Me, I just think it helps the story of Aronnax read better. Nemo's is another story entirely. Assuming I get around to it (and for *that* I have far more radical ideas, probably).

Sometimes a story can survive being two entirely separate things. For me, it didn't work with *Twenty Thousand Leagues*. I loved the opening act far too much, and was too little engaged in the rest of it to be able to reconcile it. Nemo *is* an interesting character, but he can only ever be disappointing with such a great setup, so relatively brief, and so much time given to a man who really doesn't have much of interest except his obsession that's counteracted by his self-imposed exile. Why even bother with the outside world? That's the biggest question, especially in a post-9/11 world. Is Nemo even much of a hero? Was he *always* an antihero? Was he a *villain*?

Aronnax's purely scientific interests aren't so ambiguous. He exists in a world of concrete truths, in which it's still possible to evoke mythical creature, even to use the term "unicorn" with a straight face, still attempting to justify it even though everyone knows what it really was all along. For Aronnax, and Verne, Moby-Dick isn't just the subject of Ahab's wrath, but part of a whole cast of creatures haunting the deep, in a past receding into myth, in a world coming into its own, at a crossroads, the last of an era, the beginning of another.

So all I really want is to rescue *Twenty Thousand Leagues* from relative obscurity, for it to finally claim its rightful place as a pivotal moment in literature. All I had to do was jettison its most famous element. So it could be known for something else.

A TIMELINE OF EVENTS

- July 20, 1866—the steamer *Governor Higginson* encounters mysterious oceanic entity
- July 23, 1866—the *Columbus* encounters mysterious oceanic entity
- August 7, 1866—the *Helvetia* and *Shannon* encounter mysterious oceanic entity; additional reports from the *Pereira*, *Etna*, *Normandie*, and *Lord Clyde*
- 1866—six months of hot international debate concerning the nature of mysterious oceanic entity
- 1867—opening months feature

rapid cooling of interest

- March 5, 1867—the *Moravian* becomes latest vessel to encounter mysterious oceanic entity
- April 13, 1867—the *Scotia* encounters mysterious oceanic entity; becomes definitive incident to motivate a full-scale investigation; Aronnax, having arrived in New York at the end of March, resolves to participate
- April 30, 1867—Aronnax publishes his formal thoughts on the matter
- June 2, 1867—a fresh report of sighting the mysterious oceanic entity by a steamer arrives as preparations for the *Abraham Lincoln* to launch its investigation under Commander Farragut begin; Aronnax is formally requested to take part in the adventure, and very rapidly accepts as the crew sets off shortly
- June 30, 1867—*Abraham Lincoln* consults with the whaler *Monroe* about mysterious oceanic entity
- July 3, 1867—*Abraham Lincoln* rounds Cape Horn as its journey continues
- July 6, 1867—crew of *Abraham Lincoln* still optimistic about chances for success
- July 20, 1867—*Abraham Lincoln*

- reaches Tropic of Capricorn
- July 30, 1867—*Abraham Lincoln* crosses the equator
- 1867—three months of fruitless cruising
- November 2, 1867—Farragut responds to restless crew by promising three more days of search before turning back
- November 5, 1867—harpooner Ned Land catches sight of mysterious oceanic entity, and the pursuit begins!
- November 6, 1867—eager pursuit continues; Aronnax falls overboard, followed rapidly by manservant Conseil in attempted rescue
- November 7, 1867—Aronnax and Conseil discover Ned Land also marooned in the sea, who affects their rescue after a long night treading water in hope of *Abraham Lincoln* spotting them; discovery that they have struck upon mysterious oceanic entity; first contact with inhabitants of vessel entity has proven to be
- 1869—*Twenty Thousand Leagues Under the Sea*, in the real world, begins original publication in France

www.ingramcontent.com/pod-product-compliance
Lightning Source LLC
Chambersburg PA
CBHW070005180726

48002CB00019B/2399